POE[M]
TO FALL IN
LOVE WITH

CHOSEN AND ILLUSTRATED BY
Chris Riddell

LOVE

POEMS
TO
FALL
IN
LOVE
WITH

MACMILLAN

First published 2019 by Macmillan Children's Books

This paperback edition published 2021 by Macmillan Children's Books
an imprint of Pan Macmillan
The Smithson, 6 Briset Street, London EC1M 5NR
Associated companies throughout the world
www.panmacmillan.com

ISBN 978-1-5290-2325-1

Printed and bound by CPI Group (UK) Ltd, Croydon CR0 4YY

Contents

My Life Closed Twice

LOVE AND FRIENDSHIP

Love and Friendship

Love is like the wild rose briar,
Friendship, like the holly tree
The holly is dark when the rose briar blooms,
But which will bloom most constantly?

The wild rose briar is sweet in spring,
Its summer blossoms scent the air
Yet wait till winter comes again
And who will call the wild-briar fair?

Then scorn the silly rose-wreath now
And deck thee with the holly's sheen
That when December blights thy brow
He still may leave thy garland green –

Emily Brontë

Locks

We owe it to each other to tell stories,
as people simply, not as father and daughter.
I tell it to you for the hundredth time:

'*There was a little girl, called Goldilocks,*
for her hair was long and golden,
and she was walking in the Wood and she saw – '

'*– cows.*' You say it with certainty,
remembering the strayed heifers we saw in the woods
behind the house, last month.

'Well, yes, perhaps she saw cows,
but also she saw a house.'

'– a great big house,' you tell me.

'No, a little house, all painted, neat and tidy.'

'A great big house.'

You have the conviction of all two-year-olds.
I wish I had such certitude.

'Ah. Yes. A great big house.
And she went in . . .'

6

I remember, as I tell it, that the locks
Of Southey's heroine had silvered with age.
The Old Woman and the Three Bears . . .
Perhaps they had been golden once, when she was a child.

And now, we are already up to the porridge,
'*And it was too –* '
'– hot!'
'And it was too– '
'– *cold!*'
And then it was, we chorus, '*just right.*'

8

The porridge is eaten, the baby's chair is shattered,
Goldilocks goes upstairs, examines beds, and sleeps,
unwisely.

But then the bears return.
Remembering Southey still, I do the voices:
Father Bear's gruff boom scares you, and you delight in it.

When I was a small child and heard the tale,
if I was anyone I was Baby Bear,
my porridge eaten, and my chair destroyed,
my bed inhabited by some strange girl.

You giggle when I do the baby's wail,
'Someone's been eating my porridge, and they've eaten it –'
'All up,' you say. A response it is,
Or an amen.

The bears go upstairs hesitantly,
their house now feels desecrated. They realize
what locks are for. They reach the bedroom.

'Someone's been sleeping in my bed.'
And here I hesitate, echoes of old jokes,
soft-core cartoons, crude headlines, in my head.

One day your mouth will curl at that line.
A loss of interest, later, innocence.
Innocence, as if it were a commodity.

'And if I could,' my father wrote to me,
huge as a bear himself, when I was younger,
'I would dower you with experience, without experience,'
and I, in my turn, would pass that on to you.
But we make our own mistakes. We sleep
unwisely.
It is our right.
The repetition echoes down the years.
When your children grow, when your dark locks begin to silver,
when you are an old woman, alone with your three bears,
what will you see? What stories will you tell?

'*And then Goldilocks jumped out of the window and she ran –* '
Together, now: '*All the way home.*'

And then you say, '*Again. Again. Again.*'

We owe it to each other to tell stories.

Neil Gaiman

Postcards From The Hedgehog

i.

Dear Mum,

Beautiful weather.
I saw a fox last night,
did as you always said
and rolled into a ball.
After a while it went away.
I was a bit scared all the same.
Wish you were here,

love Simon.

ii.

Dear Mum,

Lovely weather today.
Just saw a really pretty girl.
Not sure how to approach her.
She makes me really shy
but just all warm inside.
I rolled up into a ball.
Wish you were here,

love Simon.

iii.

Dear Mum,

It's raining today. I ate a slug.
Wasn't as good as the ones
you used to give us.
Tomorrow I think I'll approach the girl.
Perhaps I'll take her a slug.
She makes me ever so nervous.
I rolled up into a ball.
Wish you were here,

love Simon.

iv.

Dear Mum,

Sun's come out again.
This morning I was very brave
and I went to see her.
I edged up very carefully as you suggested,
but when I spoke to her
I discovered she was actually a pine-cone.
I felt very embarrassed.
Rolled up into a ball.
Wish you were here,

love Simon.

A. F. Harrold

La Belle Dame sans Merci

O what can ail thee, knight-at-arms,
  Alone and palely loitering?
The sedge has withered from the lake,
  And no birds sing.

O what can ail thee, knight-at-arms,
  So haggard and so woe-begone?
The squirrel's granary is full,
  And the harvest's done.

I see a lily on thy brow
    With anguish moist and fever dew;
And on thy cheek a fading rose
    Fast withereth too.

I met a lady in the meads,
    Full beautiful – a faery's child,
Her hair was long, her foot was light,
    And her eyes were wild.

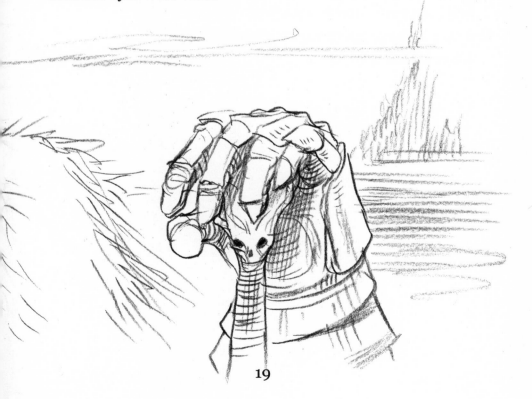

19

I made a garland for her head,
    And bracelets too, and fragrant zone;
She looked at me as she did love,
    And made sweet moan.

I set her on my pacing steed
    And nothing else saw all day long,
For sideways would she lean, and sing
    A faery's song.

She found me roots of relish sweet,
    And honey wild and manna dew,
And sure in language strange she said –
    'I love thee true'.

She took me to her elfin grot
    And there she wept and sigh'd full sore,
And there I shut her wild, wild eyes
    With kisses four.

And there she lulled me asleep,
    And there I dream'd – Ah! woe betide!
The latest dream I ever dream'd
    On the cold hill side.

I saw pale kings and princes too,
   Pale warriors, death-pale were they all;
Who cried – 'La Belle Dame sans Merci
   Hath thee in thrall!'

I saw their starved lips in the gloam
   With horrid warning gaped wide,
And I awoke and found me here
   On the cold hill's side.

And this is why I sojourn here
   Alone and palely loitering,
Though the sedge is withered from the lake,
   And no birds sing.

John Keats

23

The Beautiful Librarians

The beautiful librarians are dead,
The fairly recent graduates who sat
Like Françoise Hardy's shampooed sisters
With cardigans across their shoulders
On quiet evenings at the issue desk,
Stamping books and never looking up
At where I stood in adoration.

Once I glimpsed the staffroom
Where they smoked and (if the novels
Were correct) would speak of men.
I still see the blue Minis they would drive
Back to their flats around the park,
To Blossom Dearie and red wine
Left over from a party I would never

24

Be a member of. Their rooms looked down
On dimming avenues of lime.
I shared the geography but not the world
It seemed they were establishing
With such unfussy self-possession, nor
The novels they were writing secretly
That somehow turned to 'Mum's old stuff'.

Never to even brush in passing
Yet nonetheless keep faith with them,
The ice queens in their realms of gold –
It passes time that passes anyway.
Book after book I kept my word
Elsewhere, long after they were gone
And all the brilliant stock was sold.

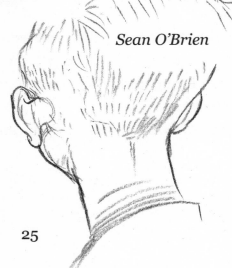

Sean O'Brien

25

Sisters of Mercy

Oh the sisters of mercy, they are not departed or gone.
They were waiting for me when I thought that I just can't go on.
And they brought me their comfort and later they brought me
    this song.
Oh I hope you run into them, you who've been travelling so long.

Yes you who must leave everything that you cannot control.
It begins with your family, but soon it comes around to your soul.
Well I've been where you're hanging, I think I can see how
    you're pinned:
When you're not feeling holy, your loneliness says that you've
    sinned.

Well they lay down beside me, I made my confession to them.
They touched both my eyes and I touched the dew on their hem.
If your life is a leaf that the seasons tear off and condemn
They will bind you with love that is graceful and green as a stem.

28

When I left they were sleeping, I hope you run into them soon.
Don't turn on the lights, you can read their address by the moon.
And you won't make me jealous if I hear that they sweetened
    your night:
We weren't lovers like that and besides it would still be all right,
We weren't lovers like that and besides it would still be all right

Leonard Cohen

29

Wormwood

mama, remember your cool hand
on mine, remember, I was twelve
and consumed with thinness.

remember you lay beside me
on the starchy sheets and talked
about healing, about your own

mother, how you became
a kite, straining away from her.
about the summer your hair

knotted up like moss
in the shower drain, mama,
remember I asked you why

you decided to live, and remember,
you pressed your fingers
gentle against my forehead,

remember, you spoke
in a low voice about the chapel
ringing with sound,

the amber light streaming
through the windows,
you told me you cried. I cried

with your arms wrapped
around my back. I cried
because the body can never

forget. mama, I cried because
I can never forget that winter,
the winter the body I tried

to carve out of marble became glass,
the winter I held death in
my mouth and proclaimed myself

full.

Margot Armbruster

You: An Achilles apple

Blushing sweet on a high branch
At the tip of the tallest tree you escaped
Those that they did not try, no.
They could not forget you
Poised beyond their reach.

Sappho

32

33

BEGINNINGS

[It's no use / Mother dear. . .]

It's no use

Mother dear, I
can't finish my
weaving
　　　You may
blame Aphrodite

soft as she is

she has almost
killed me with
love for that boy

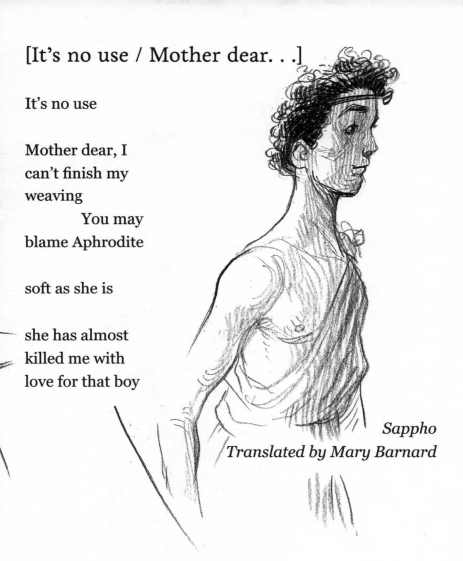

Sappho
Translated by Mary Barnard

64 Squares

I'll never understand the rules of chess
or boys. I only know the word checkmate.
Perhaps that's why my love life is a mess.

I haven't learnt the moves, it's all a guess.
My instinct is to play my bishop straight.
I'll never understand the rules of chess.

I've had beginner's luck – though I confess
my strategies are weak, I don't notate.
Perhaps that's why my love life is a mess.

I know a Kasparov – but I digress.
I send my queen towards her captured fate.
I'll never understand the rules of chess.

A game? A sport? To me, it's simply stress.
I'd rather Scrabble or Articulate.
Perhaps that's why my love life is a mess.

I gently tip my tired king to rest
and stop the clock. I'm choosing not to date.
I'll never understand the rules of chess.
Perhaps that's why my love life is a mess.

Rachel Rooney

39

She Walks in Beauty

I

She walks in beauty, like the night
  Of cloudless climes and starry skies;
And all that's best of dark and bright
  Meet in her aspect and her eyes:
Thus mellow'd to that tender light
  Which heaven to gaudy day denies.

41

II

One shade the more, one ray the less,
  Had half impair'd the nameless grace
Which waves in every raven tress,
  Or softly lightens o'er her face;
Where thoughts serenely sweet express
  How pure, how dear their dwelling place.

III

And on that cheek, and o'er that brow,
  So soft, so calm, yet eloquent,
The smiles that win, the tints that glow,
  But tell of days in goodness spent,
A mind at peace with all below,
  A heart whose love is innocent!

George Gordon, Lord Byron

43

From Romeo and Juliet

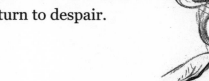

ROMEO If I profane with my unworthiest hand
  This holy shrine, the gentle sin is this:
  My lips, two blushing pilgrims, ready stand
  To smooth that rough touch with a tender kiss.

JULIET Good pilgrim, you do wrong your hand too much.
  Which mannerly devotion shows in this,
  For saints have hands that pilgrims' hands do touch,
  And palm to palm is holy palmers' kiss.

ROMEO Have not saints lips, and holy palmers too?

JULIET Ay, pilgrim, lips that they must use in prayer.

ROMEO O, then, dear saint, let lips do what hands do:
  They pray, grant thou, lest faith turn to despair.

JULIET Saints do not move, though grant for
    prayers' sake.

ROMEO Then move not, while my prayer's effect I take.
    Thus from my lips, by thine, my sin is purged.

JULIET Then have my lips the sin that they have took.

ROMEO Sin from my lips? O, trespass sweetly urged!
    Give me my sin again.

JULIET You kiss by th'book.

William Shakespeare

The Indian Serenade

I arise from dreams of thee
In the first sweet sleep of night,
When the winds are breathing low,
And the stars are shining bright:
I arise from dreams of thee,
And a spirit in my feet
Hath led me—who knows how?
To thy chamber window, Sweet!

The wandering airs they faint
On the dark, the silent stream—
The Champak odours fail
Like sweet thoughts in a dream;
The Nightingale's complaint,
It dies upon her heart;—
As I must on thine,
Oh, belovèd as thou art!

Oh lift me from the grass!
I die! I faint! I fail!
Let thy love in kisses rain
On my lips and eyelids pale.
My cheek is cold and white, alas!
My heart beats loud and fast;—
Oh! press it to thine own again,
Where it will break at last.

Percy Bysshe Shelley

47

A small dragon

I've found a small dragon in the woodshed.
Think it must have come from deep inside a forest
because it's damp and green and leaves
are still reflecting in its eyes.

I fed it on many things, tried grass,
the roots of stars, hazel-nut and dandelion,
but it stared up at me as if to say, I need
food you can't provide.

It made a nest among the coal,
not unlike a bird's but larger,
it is out of place here
and is quite silent.

If you believed in it I would come
hurrying to your house to let you share my wonder,
but I want instead to see
if you yourself will pass this way.

Brian Patten

A Lost Language

There is a language on my tongue
that I didn't even know lived there.
I call it by your love, I call it you.

It is all the softness
I learned about you
and all the seconds you meant to me.

Tell me how to untangle
and unlanguage you
from my lips

when my you
are caught on my tongue
in every single word I speak.

Nikita Gill

The Orange

At lunchtime I bought a huge orange –
The size of it made us all laugh.
I peeled it and shared it with Robert and Dave –
They got quarters and I had a half.
And that orange, it made me so happy,
As ordinary things often do
Just lately. The shopping. A walk in the park.
This is peace and contentment. It's new.
The rest of the day was quite easy.
I did all the jobs on my list
And enjoyed them and had some time over.
I love you. I'm glad I exist.

Wendy Cope

VALENTINE

Valentine

My heart has made its mind up
And I'm afraid it's you.
Whatever you've got lined up,
My heart has made its mind up
And if you can't be signed up
This year, next year will do.
My heart has made its mind up
And I'm afraid it's you.

Wendy Cope

A Valentine

Very fine is my valentine.
Very fine and very mine.
Very mine is my valentine very mine and very fine.
Very fine is my valentine and mine,
Very fine very mine and mine is my valentine.

Gertrude Stein

55

Red Boots On

Way down Geneva,
All along the Vine,
Deeper than the snow drift
Love's eyes shine

Mary Lou's Walking
In the winter time.

She's got

Red boots on, she's got
Red boots on,
Kicking up the winter
Till the winter's gone.

So

Go by Ontario,
Look down Main,
If you can't find Mary Lou,
Come back again.

Sweet light burning
In winter's flame.

She's got

Snow in her eyes, got
A tingle in her toes
And new red boots on
Wherever she goes

So

All around Lake Street,
Up by St Paul,
Quicker than the white wind
Love takes all.

Mary Lou's walking
In the big snow fall.

She's got

Red boots on, she's got
Red boots on,
Kicking up the winter
Till the winter's gone.

Kit Wright

i carry your heart with me

i carry your heart with me(i carry it in
my heart)i am never without it(anywhere
i go you go,my dear;and whatever is done
by only me is your doing,my darling)
                              i fear
no fate(for you are my fate,my sweet)i want
no world(for beautiful you are my world,my true)
and it's you are whatever a moon has always meant
and whatever a sun will always sing is you

here is the deepest secret nobody knows
(here is the root of the root and the bud of the bud
and the sky of the sky of a tree called life;which grows
higher than soul can hope or mind can hide)
and this is the wonder that's keeping the stars apart

i carry your heart(i carry it in my heart)

E. E. Cummings

'Doubt thou the stars are fire'
from Hamlet

Doubt thou the stars are fire,
Doubt that the sun doth move,
Doubt truth to be a liar,
But never doubt I love.

William Shakespeare

A Red, Red Rose

My luve is like a red, red rose,
    That's newly sprung in June:
My luve is like the melodie,
    That's sweetly play'd in tune.
As fair art thou, my bonnie lass,
    So deep in luve am I,
And I will luve thee still, my dear,
    Till a' the seas gang dry.
Till a' the seas gang dry, my dear,
    And the rocks melt wi' the sun!
And I will luve thee still, my dear,
    While the sands o' life shall run.
And fare-thee-weel, my only luve,
    And fare-thee-weel a while!
And I will come again, my luve,
    Tho' it were ten thousand mile.

Robert Burns

63

The Licorice Fields at Pontefract

In the licorice fields at Pontefract
    My love and I did meet
And many a burdened licorice bush
    Was blooming round our feet;
Red hair she had and golden skin,
Her sulky lips were shaped for sin,
Her sturdy legs were flannel-slack'd,
The strongest legs in Pontefract.

The light and dangling licorice flowers
    Gave off the sweetest smells;
From various black Victorian towers
    The Sunday evening bells
Came pealing over dales and hills
And tanneries and silent mills
And lowly streets where country stops
And little shuttered corner shops.

66

She cast her blazing eyes on me
   And plucked a licorice leaf;
I was her captive slave and she
   My red-haired robber chief.
Oh love! for love I could not speak,
It left me winded, wilting, weak
And held in brown arms strong and bare
And wound with flaming ropes of hair.

John Betjeman

Mad Girl's Love Song

I shut my eyes and all the world drops dead;
I lift my lids and all is born again.
(I think I made you up inside my head.)

The stars go waltzing out in blue and red,
And arbitrary blackness gallops in:
I shut my eyes and all the world drops dead.

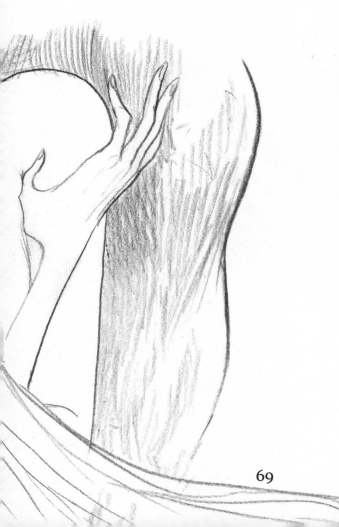

I dreamed that you bewitched me into bed
And sung me moon-struck, kissed me quite insane.
(I think I made you up inside my head.)

God topples from the sky, hell's fires fade:
Exit seraphim and Satan's men:
I shut my eyes and all the world drops dead.

I fancied you'd return the way you said,
But I grow old and I forget your name.
(I think I made you up inside my head.)

I should have loved a thunderbird instead,
At least when spring comes they roar back again.
I shut my eyes and all the world drops dead.

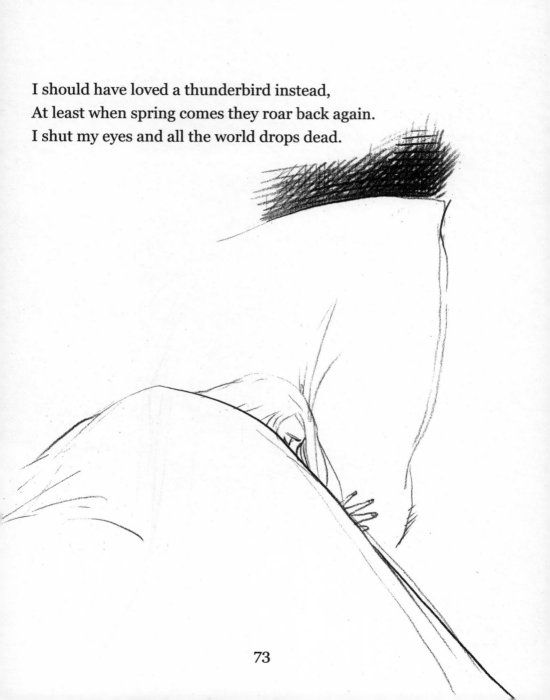

74

(I think I made you up inside my head.)

Sylvia Plath

Firework

The new woman arrived in my life
Like a fire arrives in wet woodland

I was a cave in the dirt
full of claggy old timber

She was the spark

We struggled to take
We couldn't quite catch

But every so often, with enough close attention
Our fire would roar with great authority
And light up the whole sorry place

Kate Tempest

77

Wild nights – Wild nights!

Wild nights – Wild nights!
Were I with thee
Wild nights should be
Our luxury!

Futile – the winds –
To a Heart in port –
Done with the Compass –
Done with the Chart!

Rowing in Eden –
Ah – the Sea!
Might I but moor – tonight –
In thee!

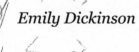

Emily Dickinson

79

Into My Arms

I don't believe in an Interventionist God
But I know, darling, that you do
But if I did I would kneel down and ask Him
Not to intervene when it came to you
Not to touch a hair on your head
To leave you as you are
And if He felt He had to direct you
Then direct you into my arms

Into my arms, O Lord
Into my arms, O Lord
Into my arms, O Lord
Into my arms

81

And I don't believe in the existence of angels
But looking at you I wonder if that's true
But if I did I would summon them together
And ask them to watch over you
To each burn a candle for you
To make bright and clear your path
And to walk, like Christ, in grace and love
And guide you into my arms

Into my arms, O Lord
Into my arms, O Lord
Into my arms, O Lord
Into my arms

83

And I believe in Love
And I know that you do too
And I believe in some kind of path
That we can walk down, me and you
So keep your candles burning
And make her journey bright and pure
That she will keep returning
Always and evermore

Into my arms, O Lord
Into my arms, O Lord
Into my arms, O Lord
Into my arms

Nick Cave

Words, Wide Night

Somewhere on the other side of this wide night
and the distance between us, I am thinking of you.
The room is turning slowly away from the moon.

This is pleasurable. Or shall I cross that out and say
it is sad? In one of the tenses I singing
an impossible song of desire that you cannot hear.

La lala la. See? I close my eyes and imagine
the dark hills I would have to cross
to reach you. For I am in love with you and this

is what it is like or what it is like in words.

Carol Ann Duffy

87

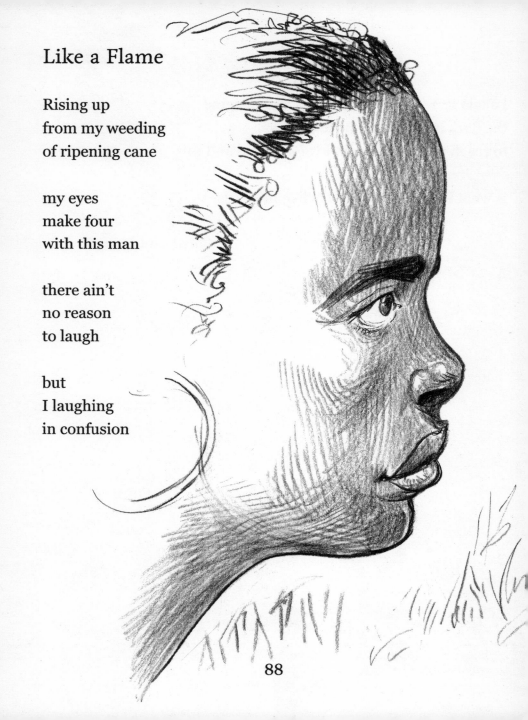

Like a Flame

Rising up
from my weeding
of ripening cane

my eyes
make four
with this man

there ain't
no reason
to laugh

but
I laughing
in confusion

88

his hands
soft his words
quick his lips
curling as in
prayer

I nod

I like this man

tonight
I go to meet him
like a flame

Grace Nichols

dolores

I'm watching you as I pull
sand from my skin,
tiny studs who balk at their fate —
and I want you to move,
sift your hands through mine
as if we were easy that way.
the sea ticks out a drumbeat
and all my limbs stick in their sockets.

later we will climb the grimy walls
along with the ivy;
you will shrug your shoulders, tar-slow,
beneath a grinning yellow street lamp.
later I will whisper to you.
under the Spanish moon,
the things I would let you do to me.

Priya Bryant

LET'S STICK TOGETHER

Like Otters

maybe there's no fear
that we'll float far apart
from each other
in these waters
as moon beckons tide

but cosy in bed, still
i rest so much better,
like otters, together
your hand warm in mine

Hollie McNish

Wedding Thoughts: All I Know About Love

This is everything I have to tell you about love: *nothing*.
This is everything I've learned about marriage: *nothing*.

Only that the world out there is complicated,
and there are beasts in the night, and delight and pain,
and the only thing that makes it okay, sometimes,
is to reach out a hand in the darkness and find another hand
    to squeeze,
and not to be alone.

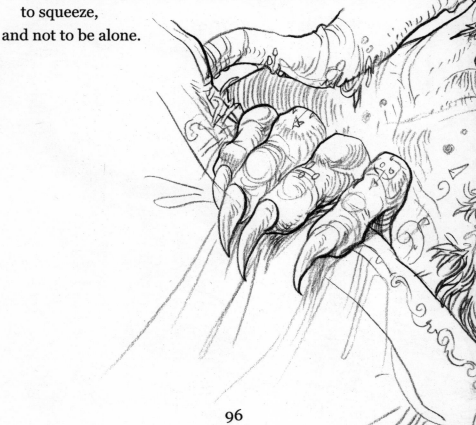

It's not the kisses, or never just the kisses: it's what they mean.
Somebody's got your back.
Somebody knows your worst self and somehow doesn't want to
     rescue you
or send for the army to rescue them.

It's not two broken halves becoming one.
It's the light from a distant lighthouse bringing you both safely
   home
because home is wherever you are both together.

So this is everything I have to tell you about love and marriage:
   nothing,
like a book without pages or a forest without trees.

Because there are things you cannot know before you experience
   them.
Because no study can prepare you for the joys or the trials.
Because nobody else's love, nobody else's marriage, is like yours,
and it's a road you can only learn by walking it,
a dance you cannot be taught,
a song that did not exist before you began, together, to sing.

And because in the darkness you will reach out a hand,
not knowing for certain if someone else is even there.
And your hands will meet,
and then neither of you will ever need to be alone again.

And that's all I know about love.

Neil Gaiman

happiness

lying in bed ofa weekdaymorning
Autumn
and the trees
none the worse for it.
Youve just got up
to make tea toast and a bottle
leaving pastures warm
for me to stretch into

in his cot
the littlefella
outsings the birds

Plenty of honey in the cupboard.
Nice.

Roger McGough

The Bargain

My true love hath my heart, and I have his,
  By just exchange one for another given:
I hold his dear, and mine he cannot miss,
  There never was a better bargain driven:
    My true love hath my heart, and I have his.

His heart in me keeps him and me in one,
  My heart in him his thoughts and senses guides:
He loves my heart, for once it was his own,
  I cherish his because in me it bides:
    My true love hath my heart, and I have his.

Sir Philip Sidney

'Faith, hope and love'

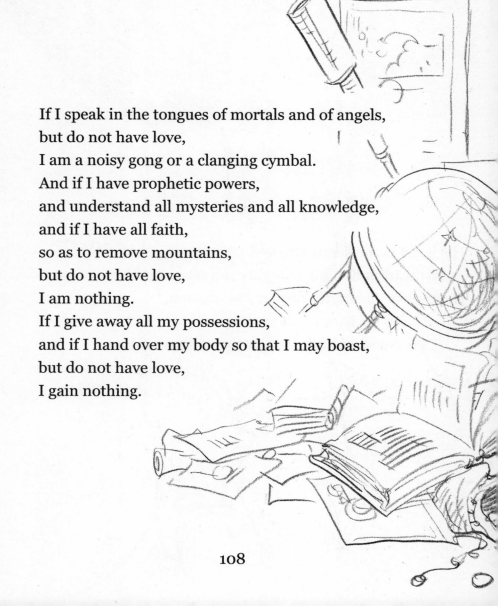

If I speak in the tongues of mortals and of angels,
but do not have love,
I am a noisy gong or a clanging cymbal.
And if I have prophetic powers,
and understand all mysteries and all knowledge,
and if I have all faith,
so as to remove mountains,
but do not have love,
I am nothing.
If I give away all my possessions,
and if I hand over my body so that I may boast,
but do not have love,
I gain nothing.

110

Love is patient;
love is kind;
love is not envious or boastful or arrogant or rude.
It does not insist on its own way;
it is not irritable or resentful;
it does not rejoice in wrongdoings,
but rejoices in the truth.
It bears all things,
believes all things,
hopes all things,
endures all things.

Love never ends.
But as for prophecies,
they will come to an end;
as for tongues,
they will cease;
as for knowledge,
it will come to an end.
For we know only in part,
and we prophesy only in part;
but when the complete comes,
the partial will come to an end.

113

When I was a child,
I spoke like a child,
I thought like a child,
I reasoned like a child;
when I became an adult,
I put an end to childish ways.
For now we see in a mirror, dimly,
but then we will see face to face.
Now I know only in part;
then I will know fully,
even as I have been fully known.
And now faith, hope, and love abide, these three;

and the greatest of these is love.

1 Corinthians 13:1–13

116

Sonnet 116

Let me not to the marriage of true minds
Admit impediments. Love is not love
Which alters when it alteration finds,
Or bends with the remover to remove:
O, no, it is an ever-fixed mark,
That looks on tempests and is never shaken;
It is the star to every wandering bark,
Whose worth's unknown, although his height be taken.
Love's not Time's fool, though rosy lips and cheeks
Within his bending sickle's compass come;
Love alters not with his brief hours and weeks,
But bears it out even to the edge of doom.
    If this be error and upon me proved,
    I never writ, nor no man ever loved.

William Shakespeare

117

The Owl and the Pussy-Cat

The Owl and the Pussy-Cat went to sea
In a beautiful pea-green boat.
They took some honey, and plenty of money
Wrapped up in a five-pound note.

The Owl looked up to the stars above,
And sang to a small guitar,
'O lovely Pussy! O Pussy, my love,
What a beautiful Pussy you are,
You are,
You are!
What a beautiful Pussy you are!'

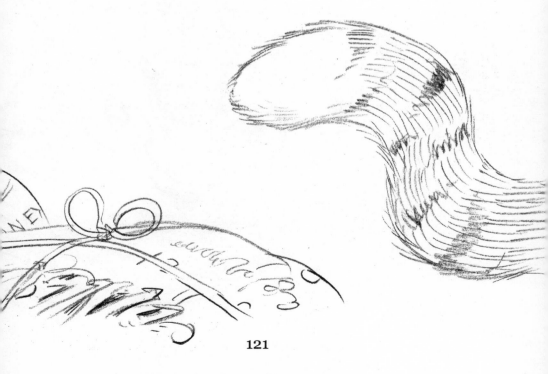

Pussy said to the Owl, 'You elegant fowl!
How charmingly sweet you sing!
O let us be married! too long we have tarried:
But what shall we do for a ring?'
They sailed away, for a year and a day,
To the land where the Bong-Tree grows,

And there in a wood a Piggy-wig stood.
With a ring at the end of his nose,
His nose,
His nose!
With a ring at the end of his nose.

'Dear Pig, are you willing to sell for one shilling
Your ring?' Said the Piggy, 'I will.'
So they took it away, and were married next day
By the turkey who lives on the hill.

They dined on mince, and slices of quince,
Which they ate with a runcible spoon;
And hand in hand, on the edge of the sand
They danced by the light of the moon,
The moon,
The moon,
They danced by the light of the moon.

Edward Lear

'How do I love thee?'
(*Sonnets from the Portuguese, XLIII*)

How do I love thee? Let me count the ways.
I love thee to the depth and breadth and height
My soul can reach, when feeling out of sight
For the ends of Being and ideal Grace.
I love thee to the level of everyday's
Most quiet need, by sun and candle-light.
I love thee freely, as men strive for Right:
I love thee purely, as they turn from Praise.
I love thee with the passion put to use
In my old griefs, and with my childhood's faith.
I love thee with a love I seemed to lose
With my lost saints! – I love thee with the breath,
Smiles, tears, of all my life! – and, if God choose,
I shall but love thee better after death.

Elizabeth Barrett Browning

127

The Good-Morrow

I wonder, by my troth, what thou and I
Did, till we loved? Were we not weaned till then?
But sucked on country pleasures, childishly?
Or snorted we in the Seven Sleepers' den?
'Twas so; but this, all pleasures fancies be.
If ever any beauty I did see,
Which I desired, and got, 'twas but a dream of thee.

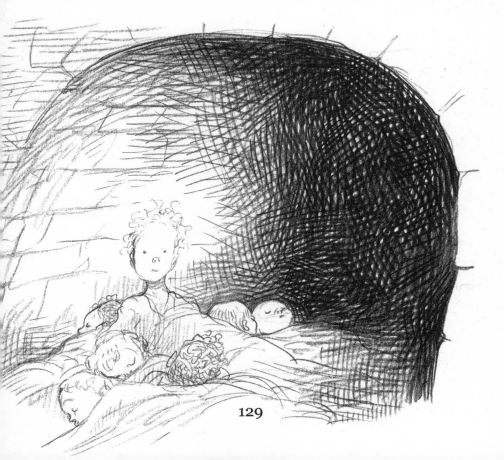

129

And now good-morrow to our waking souls,
Which watch not one another out of fear;
For love, all love of other sights controls,
And makes one little room an everywhere.
Let sea-discoverers to new worlds have gone,
Let maps to other, worlds on worlds have shown,
Let us possess one world, each hath one, and is one.

My face in thine eye, thine in mine appears,
And true plain hearts do in the faces rest;
Where can we find two better hemispheres,
Without sharp north, without declining west?
Whatever dies, was not mixed equally;
If our two loves be one, or, thou and I
Love so alike, that none do slacken, none can die.

John Donne

If You Are An Ancient Egyptian Pharaoh

I am carving dirty hieroglyphics
into the wall of your tomb

If you are a dead French aristocrat
I am the suspicious circumstances
surrounding your death

If you are a shape-shifting wizard
I am the shape you are shifting into

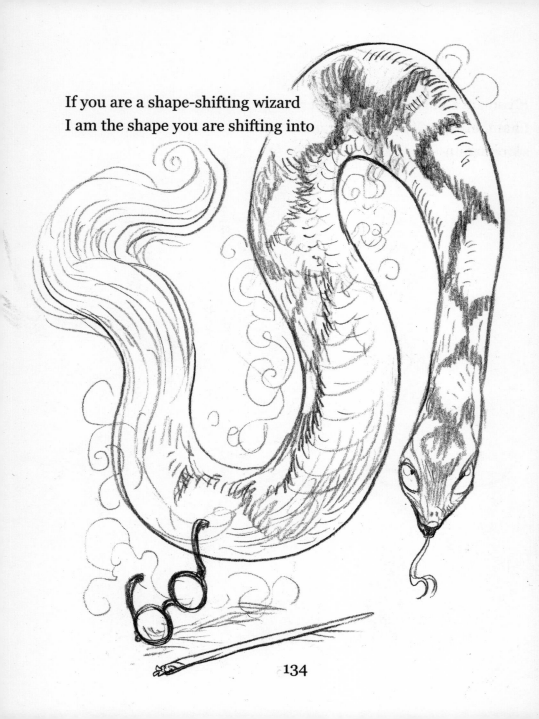

If you are a fast-moving cloud
I am an entire field of deer
looking up

If you are a sceptical cop
I am a haunted fax machine

If you are a catapult
I am the medieval knight
you are catapulting
I fly over the dark fields of my enemies
corkscrewing the dawn

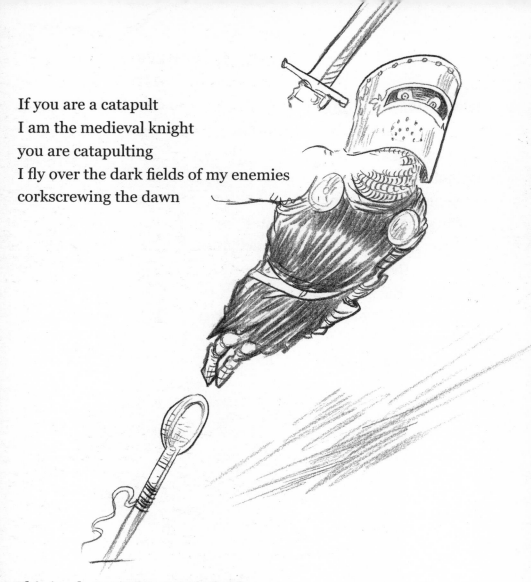

This is what missing you feels like

Without you
I am just the suspicious circumstances
surrounding nothing
Without you I am just
a regular medieval knight
settling ongoing tenancy disputes
and doing other knight-related activities
like dying thousands of years ago
I rise from the grave to lean
like an ancient wind against your house
Your roof a red eyelid
closed against the sky

138

When I'm not with you I am like
a lonely wrestler with nobody to break chairs on

When you take off your clothes
the whole room darkens to light you
Your nakedness a pale kite

141

I want to take you to the river that runs behind my house
and show you where the dark water vanishes between the rocks

but I can't
because nothing runs behind my house
not even a lonely commercial highway
I want to stand with you
on the edge of a lonely commercial highway
waiting for the jumper cables
that will restart this engine
and take us somewhere far beyond
the confines of this poem

I need to have a reason
for the aisles of trees we sailed through
and your hand on my knee in reckless disregard
of road safety recommendations

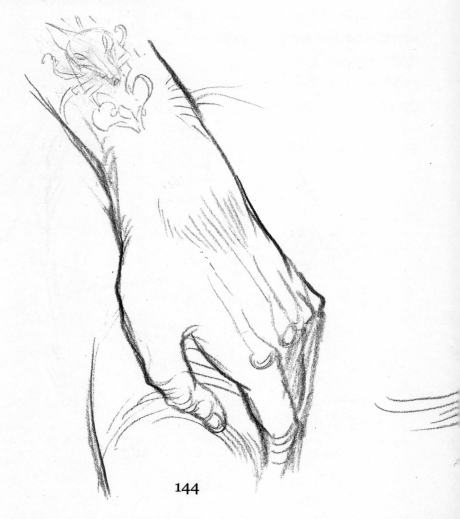

I need to have a reason
for so many nights of watching you recede from me,
like the ass end of a horse
in the credits of a Western

I need to have a reason
for drinking beer in your parents' swimming pool at night
and how you lay face down in the water
like a body in a celestial crime scene

The stars so many knives
in the small of your back

Hera Lindsay Bird

the parents anniversary

that on the last day of july
my father would tell the story
of how they had met
so young in photos i once saw
of an eighties blurred with rain
and home haircuts
how easily she had made
her impression and left it there
     that years later he would
follow her to pulsing cities
and countries now closed
to the rest of the world
     that they would marry
dress each other in light
a day so hot that sand
could boil to glass
she, a striped cat who purrs
he, a tamed bear
     that they could repeat these words

a little different year by year
but by the same stellate night
that he could sleep in
the fourth chamber of her heart
and stay there and stay there

Lucy Thynne

149

Dark Sonnet

I don't think that I've been in love as such
although I liked a few folk pretty well

Love must be vaster than my smiles or touch
for brave men died and empires rose and fell
for love, girls follow boys to foreign lands
and men have followed women into hell
In plays and poems someone understands
there's something makes us more than blood and bone

And more than biological demands for me love's like the wind
unseen, unknown
I see the trees are bending where it's been
I know that it leaves wreckage where it's blown

I really don't know what I love you means
I think it means don't leave me here alone

Neil Gaiman

153

The Song of Wandering Aengus

I went out to the hazel wood,
Because a fire was in my head,
And cut and peeled a hazel wand,
And hooked a berry to a thread;
And when white moths were on the wing,
And moth-like stars were flickering out,
I dropped the berry in a stream
And caught a little silver trout.

When I had laid it on the floor
I went to blow the fire aflame,
But something rustled on the floor,
And some one called me by my name:
It had become a glimmering girl
With apple blossom in her hair
Who called me by my name and ran
And faded through the brightening air.

Though I am old with wandering
Through hollow lands and hilly lands,
I will find out where she has gone,
And kiss her lips and take her hands;
And walk among long dappled grass,
And pluck till time and times are done
The silver apples of the moon,
The golden apples of the sun.

W. B. Yeats

155

Love After Love

The time will come
when, with elation,
you will greet yourself arriving
at your own door, in your own mirror,
and each will smile at the other's welcome,

And say, sit here. Eat.
You will love again the stranger who was yourself.
Give wine. Give bread. Give back your heart
to itself, to the stranger who has loved you

all your life, whom you ignored
for another, who knows you by heart.
Take down the love letters from the bookshelf,

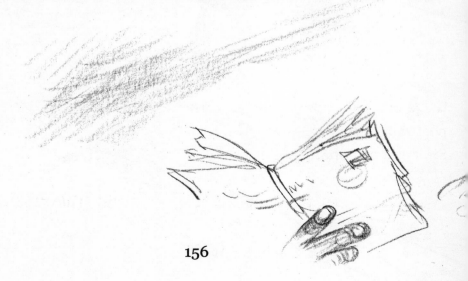

the photographs, the desperate notes,
peel your own image from the mirror.
Sit. Feast on your life.

Derek Walcott

MY LIFE
CLOSED TWICE

'My life closed twice before its close'

My life closed twice before its close –
It yet remains to see
If Immortality unveil
A third event to me

So huge, so hopeless to conceive
As these that twice befell.
Parting is all we know of heaven,
And all we need of hell.

Emily Dickinson

161

The Courtship of the Yonghy-Bonghy-Bo

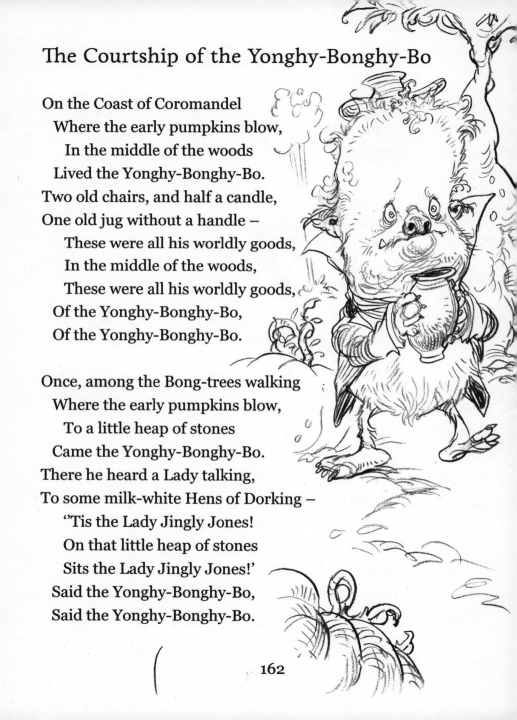

On the Coast of Coromandel
  Where the early pumpkins blow,
    In the middle of the woods
  Lived the Yonghy-Bonghy-Bo.
Two old chairs, and half a candle,
One old jug without a handle –
    These were all his worldly goods,
    In the middle of the woods,
    These were all his worldly goods,
  Of the Yonghy-Bonghy-Bo,
  Of the Yonghy-Bonghy-Bo.

Once, among the Bong-trees walking
  Where the early pumpkins blow,
    To a little heap of stones
  Came the Yonghy-Bonghy-Bo.
There he heard a Lady talking,
To some milk-white Hens of Dorking –
    ''Tis the Lady Jingly Jones!
    On that little heap of stones
    Sits the Lady Jingly Jones!'
  Said the Yonghy-Bonghy-Bo,
  Said the Yonghy-Bonghy-Bo.

162

'Lady Jingly! Lady Jingly!
  Sitting where the pumpkins blow,
    Will you come and be my wife?'
  Said the Yongby-Bonghy-Bo.
'I am tired of living singly –
On this coast so wild and shingly –
    I'm a-weary of my life;
    If you'll come and be my wife,
    Quite serene would be my life!'
  Said the Yonghy-Bongby-Bo,
  Said the Yonghy-Bonghy-Bo.

'On this Coast of Coromandel
  Shrimps and watercresses grow,
    Prawns are plentiful and cheap,'
  Said the Yonghy-Bonghy-Bo.
'You shall have my chairs and candle,
And my jug without a handle!
    Gaze upon the rolling deep
    (Fish is plentiful and cheap);
    As the sea, my love is deep!'
  Said the Yonghy-Bonghy-Bo,
  Said the Yonghy-Bonghy-Bo.

163

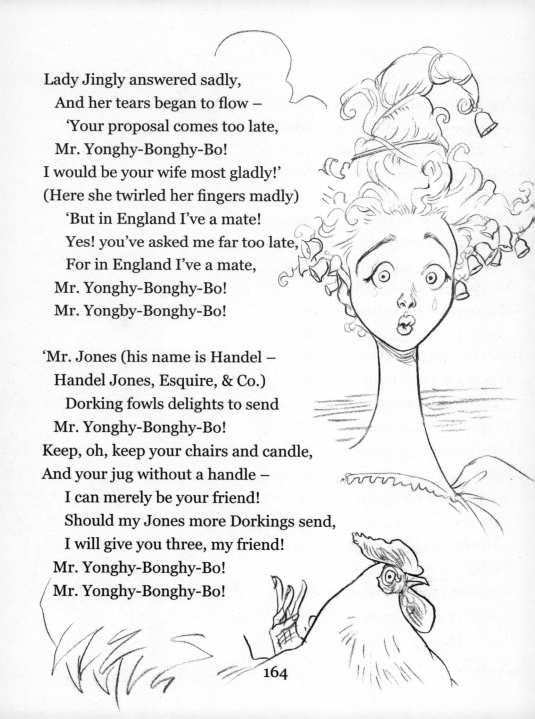

Lady Jingly answered sadly,
  And her tears began to flow –
    'Your proposal comes too late,
  Mr. Yonghy-Bonghy-Bo!
I would be your wife most gladly!'
(Here she twirled her fingers madly)
    'But in England I've a mate!
    Yes! you've asked me far too late,
    For in England I've a mate,
  Mr. Yonghy-Bonghy-Bo!
  Mr. Yongby-Bonghy-Bo!

'Mr. Jones (his name is Handel –
  Handel Jones, Esquire, & Co.)
    Dorking fowls delights to send
  Mr. Yonghy-Bonghy-Bo!
Keep, oh, keep your chairs and candle,
And your jug without a handle –
    I can merely be your friend!
    Should my Jones more Dorkings send,
    I will give you three, my friend!
  Mr. Yonghy-Bonghy-Bo!
  Mr. Yonghy-Bonghy-Bo!

'Though you've such a tiny body,
    And your head so large doth grow –
        Though your hat may blow away
    Mr. Yonghy-Bonghy-Bo!
Though you're such a Hoddy Doddy,
Yet I wish that I could modi-
        fy the words I needs must say!
        will you please to go away
            That is all I have to say,
    Mr. Yonghy-Bonghy-Bo!
    Mr. Yonghy-Bonghy-Bo!'

Down the slippery slopes of Myrtle,
    Where the early pumpkins blow,
        To the calm and silent sea
    Fled the Yonghy-Bonghy-Bo.
There, beyond the Bay of Gurtle,
Lay a large and lively Turtle.
    'You're the Cove,' he said, 'for me;
        On your back beyond the sea,
        Turtle, you shall carry me!'
    Said the Yonghy-Bonghy-Bo,
    Said the Yonghy-Bonghy-Bo.

Through the silent-roaring ocean
  Did the Turtle swiftly go;
    Holding fast upon his shell
  Rode the Yonghy-Bonghy-Bo.
With a sad primeval motion
Towards the sunset isles of Boshen
    Still the Turtle bore him well.
    Holding fast upon his shell,
    'Lady Jingly Jones, farewell!'
Sang the Yonghy-Bonghy-Bo,
Sang the Yonghy-Bonghy-Bo.

From the Coast of Coromandel
  Did that Lady never go;
    On that heap of stones she mourns
  For the Yonghy-Bonghy-Bo.
On that Coast of Coromandel,
In his jug without a handle
  Still she weeps, and daily moans;
  On that little heap of stones
  To her Dorking Hens she moans,
For the Yonghy-Bonghy-Bo,
For the Yonghy-Bonghy-Bo.

Edward Lear

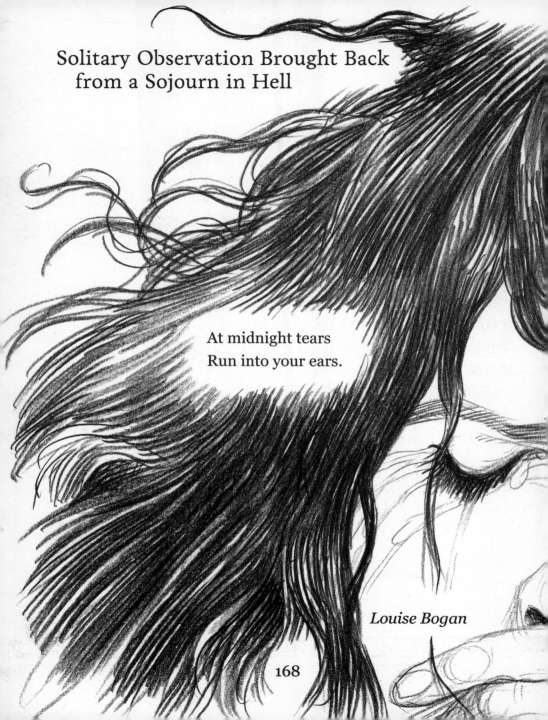

Solitary Observation Brought Back
from a Sojourn in Hell

At midnight tears
Run into your ears.

Louise Bogan

168

Me & My Dog

We had a great day
Even though we forgot to eat
And you had a bad dream
Then we got no sleep
'Cause we were kissing

I had a fever
Until I met you
Now you make me cool
But sometimes I still do
Something embarrassing

I never said I'd be all right
Just thought I could hold myself together
But I couldn't breathe, I went outside
Don't know why I thought it'd be any better
I'm fine now, it doesn't matter

I didn't wanna be this guy
I cried at your show with the teenagers
Tell your friend I'll be all right
In the morning it won't matter

I wanna be emaciated
I wanna hear one song without thinking of you
I wish I was on a spaceship
Just me and my dog and an impossible view

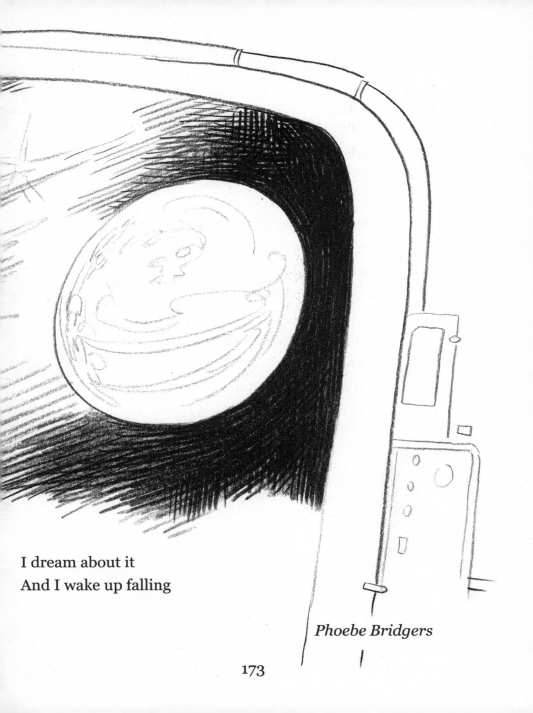

I dream about it
And I wake up falling

Phoebe Bridgers

173

The Sick Rose

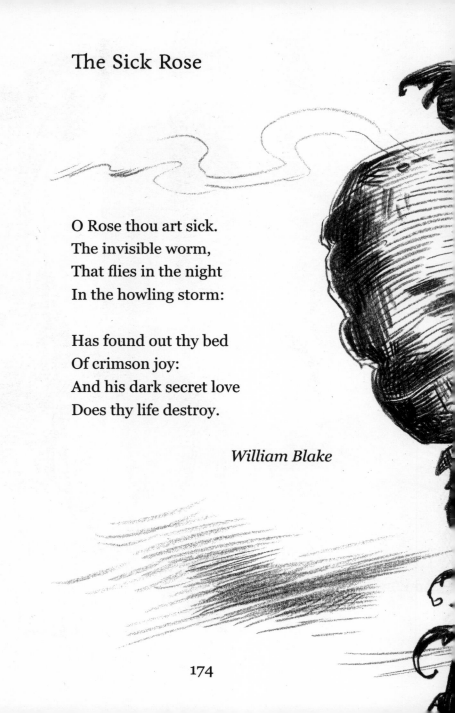

O Rose thou art sick.
The invisible worm,
That flies in the night
In the howling storm:

Has found out thy bed
Of crimson joy:
And his dark secret love
Does thy life destroy.

William Blake

175

Remember

Remember me when I am gone away,
   Gone far away into the silent land;
   When you can no more hold me by the hand,
Nor I half turn to go yet turning stay.
Remember me when no more day by day
   You tell me of our future that you plann'd:
   Only remember me; you understand
It will be late to counsel then or pray.
Yet if you should forget me for a while
   And afterwards remember, do not grieve:
   For if the darkness and corruption leave
   A vestige of the thoughts that once I had,
Better by far you should forget and smile
   Than that you should remember and be sad.

Christina Rossetti

I can't remember what we talked about

I can't remember what we talked about
But we talked all through that afternoon,
The balcony bright with sunshine behind you
As you rocked on that old rocking chair from the Watton sale rooms.
I can't remember what we talked about.

It is not your absence that fills the pockets of my heart with stones.
We were so often far apart:
In age; in experience, in geography –

Your voice on the other end of a line from
Cairo; Istanbul, Kuala Lumpur . . .
But when we talked, you were as close to me as anyone will ever be.

Nkosi Sikelel'iafrika, you loved that anthem- a stone.
Banana leaf curry, electrical storm over penang- a stone.

Hospital bed, wires, bleeps, your stubble, your toe nails still
growing, a pieta,
Our father's benediction, his hand on your brow
As you left us-
Stones, stones, stones.

But that afternoon in Florence Road
We talked and we both knew we loved
Each other though would never say as much.
That memory eases my stone heavy heart.

I can't remember what we talked about.

Chris Riddell

The Taste of a Biscuit

I remembered how I used to play with my mum.
As a kid, in the kitchen, we would bake together.

Now, though she's gone,
and although I'm grown up
and can care for myself, can cook for myself,
although I don't need her to wash my hair or buy my clothes
or hold my hand as I cross the road,
still it was nice to know she was always there, just in case.

Looking through her drawers after she'd died
I found, buried down, tucked away at one side
a little plastic thing, shaped like a star,
that I hadn't seen for twenty years or more,
that we used to use to cut biscuits from rolled out dough.

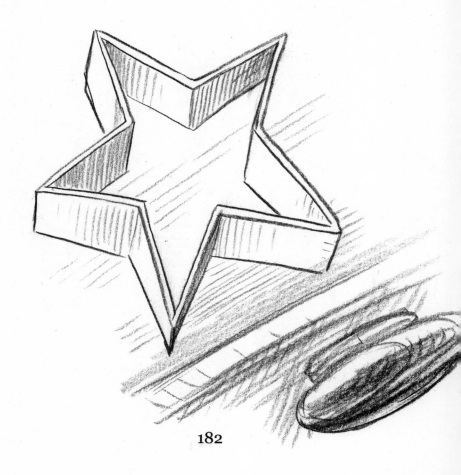

And it was just this that I remembered today,
while chatting with friends about other things.
As I took a cookie to dunk in my tea
it was as if the memory crept up on me,

and sadness came along hand in hand and hugged me.

A. F. Harrold

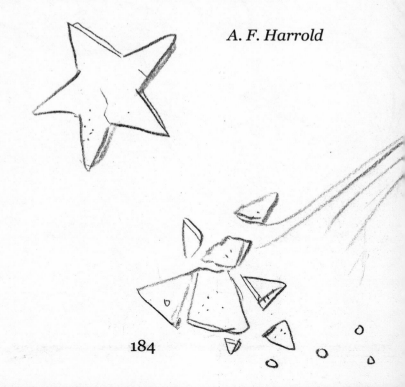

Funeral Blues

Stop all the clocks, cut off the telephone,
Prevent the dog from barking with a juicy bone,
Silence the pianos and with muffled drum
Bring out the coffin, let the mourners come.

Let aeroplanes circle moaning overhead
Scribbling on the sky the message 'He is Dead'.
Put crepe bows round the white necks of the public doves,
Let the traffic policemen wear black cotton gloves.

He was my North, my South, my East and West,
My working week and my Sunday rest,
My noon, my midnight, my talk, my song;
I thought that love would last forever: I was wrong.

The stars are not wanted now; put out every one,
Pack up the moon and dismantle the sun,
Pour away the ocean and sweep up the wood;
For nothing now can ever come to any good.

W. H. Auden

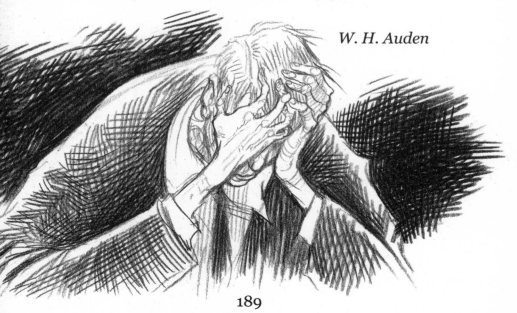

Tomorrow when you will not wake

tomorrow when you will not wake
I will do an old thing –
tomorrow when you will not wake
I will do a new

I will walk the same walk
but step it solitary –
follow the familiar path
in new pinchblack shoes

I will cook the Friday soup
with shiny orange lentils
I will simmer one brown egg
in the pan we never use

tomorrow when you will not wake
I will do an old thing
tomorrow when you will not wake
I will do a new

191

I will tear the curtains down
and burn them on a bonfire
claw the paper from the walls
scrape mortar from the bricks

I will rip the slate roof off
and fling it at the magpies
take a hammer to the chimney
and thud it through the breast

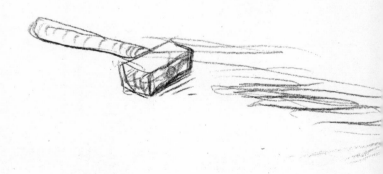

tomorrow when you will not wake
I will do an old thing
tomorrow when you will not wake
I will do a new

Jan Dean

Index of First Lines

Index of Poets

Acknowledgements

The compiler and publisher would like to thank the following for permission to use their copyright material:

Armbruster, Margot: 'Wormwood', a Foyle Young Poets of the Year award-winning poem (The Poetry Society, 2018). Copyright © The Poetry Society. Used by permission of the publisher; **Auden, W. H.:** 'Funeral Blues' from *W. H. Auden Collected* (1938). Copyright © W. H. Auden 1938, renewed. Reprinted by permission of Curtis Brown, Ltd; **Betjeman, John:** 'The Licorice Fields at Pontefract' from *Collected Poems* (John Murray, 1958) by John Betjeman. Copyright © John Betjeman 1955, 1958, 1962, 1964, 1968, 1970, 1979, 1981, 1982, 2001. Reproduced by permission of John Murray, an imprint of Hodder and Stoughton Ltd; **Bird, Hera Lindsay:** 'If You are an Ancient Egyptian Hero' from *Hera Lindsay Bird* by Hera Lindsay Bird (Penguin Books, 2017). Copyright © Hera Lindsay Bird 2017. Used with permission of Penguin Books, an imprint of Penguin Random House; **Bogan, Louise:** 'Solitary Observation Brought Back from a Sojourn in Hell' from *The Blue Estuaries* by Louise Bogan (Farrar, Straus and Giroux, 1968). Copyright © Louise Bogan 1968, renewed 1996 by Ruth Limmer. Reprinted by permission of Farrar, Straus and Giroux; **Baker, Julien**; **Bridgers, Phoebe and Dacus, Lucy:** 'Me and My Dog'. Words and Music by Julien Baker, Phoebe Bridgers and Lucy Dacus. Copyright © 2018 Big Deal Beats, Looseleaf Daykiss, Kobalt Music Services America Inc. and Whatever Mom. All Rights for Big Deal Beats and Looseleaf Daykiss Administered by Words & Music, a division of Big Deal Music Group. All Rights for Kobalt Music Services America Inc. and Whatever Mom Administered Worldwide by Kobalt Songs Music Publishing. All Rights Reserved. Reprinted by permission of Hal Leonard LLC and Kobalt Music Group Ltd.; **Bryant, Priya:** 'dolores', a Foyle Young Poets of the Year award-winning poem (The Poetry Society, 2016). Copyright © The Poetry Society. Used by permission of the publisher; **Cave, Nick:** 'Into My Arms' by Nick Cave (Mute Song Limited). Copyright © Nick Cave. Used with permission of the publisher; **Cohen, Leonard:** 'Sisters of Mercy' by Leonard Cohen. Copyright © Leonard Cohen and Leonard Cohen Stranger Music, Inc., 1993. Used by permission of The Wylie Agency (UK) Limited; **Cope, Wendy:** 'Valentine' and 'The Orange' from *Two Cures for Love* (Faber and Faber, 1992) by Wendy Cope. Copyright © Wendy Cope, 1992. Printed by permission of United Agents (www.unitedagents.co.uk) on behalf of Wendy Cope and by permission of the publisher; **Cummings, E. E.:** 'i carry your heart with me(i carry it in' from *Complete Poems: 1904-1962* by E. E. Cummings, edited by George J. Firmage. Copyright © the Trustees for the E. E. Cummings Trust, 1980, 1991. Used by permissions of Liverlight Publishing Corporation; **Dean, Jan:** 'Tomorrow when you will not wake' by Jan Dean. Copyright © Jan Dean. Used with kind permission of the author; **Duffy, Carol Ann:** 'Words,

About Chris Riddell

Chris Riddell, the 2015–2017 UK Children's Laureate, is an accomplished artist and the political cartoonist for the *Observer*. He has enjoyed great acclaim for his books for children. His books have won a number of major prizes, including the 2001, 2004 and 2016 CILIP Kate Greenaway Medals. *Goth Girl and the Ghost of a Mouse* won the Costa Children's Book Award in 2013. His previous work for Macmillan includes the bestselling Ottoline books, *The Emperor of Absurdia*, and, with Paul Stewart, Muddle Earth and the Scavenger series. Chris lives in Brighton with his family.